W9-CBL-096

OTHER YEARLING BOOKS YOU WILL ENJOY:

SOMETHING QUEER IN ROCK 'N' ROLL, *Elizabeth Levy*
SOMETHING QUEER AT THE LIBRARY, *Elizabeth Levy*
SOMETHING QUEER IS GOING ON, *Elizabeth Levy*
SOMETHING QUEER ON VACATION, *Elizabeth Levy*
SOMETHING QUEER AT THE HAUNTED SCHOOL, *Elizabeth Levy*
SOMETHING QUEER AT THE BALLPARK, *Elizabeth Levy*
CAM JANSEN AND THE MYSTERY OF THE TELEVISION DOG,
David A. Adler
THE CAT'S BURGLAR, *Peggy Parish*
THE PIZZA MONSTER, *Marjorie and Mitchell Sharmat*
THE SMALL POTATOES' BUSY BEACH DAY, *Harriet Ziefert*

YEARLING BOOKS/YOUNG YEARLINGS/YEARLING CLASSICS are designed especially to entertain and enlighten young people. Patricia Reilly Giff, consultant to this series, received her bachelor's degree from Marymount College and a master's degree in history from St. John's University. She holds a Professional Diploma in Reading and a Doctorate of Humane Letters from Hofstra University. She was a teacher and reading consultant for many years, and is the author of numerous books for young readers.

For a complete listing of all Yearling titles, write to
Dell Readers Service,
P.O. Box 1045,
South Holland, IL 60473.

Something Queer at the Lemonade Stand

by
Elizabeth Levy
illustrated by
Mordicai Gerstein

A YOUNG YEARLING BOOK

Published by
Dell Publishing
a division of
Bantam Doubleday Dell Publishing Group, Inc.
666 Fifth Avenue
New York, New York 10103

*To Mom and Dad who paid for all
those lemonades before I turned a profit.*   E.L.

ISBN: 0-440-48495-2

Reprinted by arrangement with Delacorte Press
Printed in the United States of America

June 1983

10   9

CWO

On a hot summer day Gwen and Jill decided to open a lemonade stand. They made the lemonade with fresh lemons and gave a spoonful to Fletcher. He licked it and yawned.

"It's good, but not great," said Gwen. Jill picked some mint from her window box and put it in the lemonade. They all took another taste.

Fletcher not only licked the spoon, but he licked Jill's hand and moved up her arm and licked it all over.

"Fletcher loves it!" cried Gwen. "Let's call it Fletcher's Fabulous Lemonade!"

They made a big sign, got a box, and went outside. Fletcher fell asleep in the shade.

Donald Payson, their next-door neighbor, came by, carrying a huge load of bricks and wood in the wheelbarrow. His friends, Dana and Erica Langer, were helping him.

"Lemonade!" exclaimed Donald. "Boy, can I use that!"

Gwen gave him a glass. Dana and Erica didn't want any.

Just then, Police Officer Pat Malloy came up and bought some lemonade. Dana, Erica, and Donald disappeared. "Hey, he didn't pay," said Gwen.

"We'll get him later," said Jill.

Officer Malloy took a sip and said, "This is the best lemonade I've ever had. I was dying of thirst. We're moving into our new police station around the corner, and it isn't air conditioned yet."

"Tell all your friends," said Gwen.

"I will," said Officer Malloy.

Officer Malloy was true to her word.
Soon lots of police officers walked over on
their breaks. Gwen and Jill had so many
customers they ran out of lemonade.

They went inside to make a new pitcher.

Someone knocked on their door. It was Donald, Dana, and Erica.

"I forgot to pay you this morning," said Donald.

"Thanks," said Jill. "I didn't think you'd rip us off."

"I guess you did so well, you're going to quit now and spend your money," said Erica.

"Oh, no," said Gwen. "We're just getting started. We'll keep our stand up all summer."

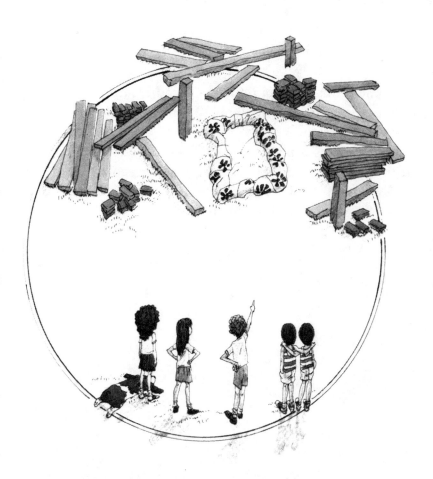

They went back outside. Jill looked at the
pile of bricks and wood in Donald's backyard. "What are you building?" she asked.

"An outside aquarium," said Donald
proudly.

"Donald has one of the best tropical-fish
collections in the city," said Erica.

"Some of his fish can do tricks," said Dana. "His Flying Angels can really jump. We told him he should charge admission."

"I'm building a platform," said Donald. "Then I'll put all my fish in my old see-through wading pool."

"Excellent," said Gwen. "When kids come to see your aquarium, we'll sell them lemonade."

The next day Gwen and Jill put out their box and sign. They went back into the house to make a bigger and even better batch of lemonade.

When everything was ready, they lugged out their lemonade and ice. Suddenly they heard a howl that started loudly and ended with a whimper. They put down the pitcher of lemonade and ran toward the sound.

They found Fletcher in a big hole. It wasn't very deep but Fletcher couldn't get out. Jill climbed down and got him.

Gwen tapped her braces. She always tapped her braces whenever something queer was going on. "I wonder how he got in there?" she asked.

Jill shrugged her shoulders. "He probably thought it was nice and cool," she said. "Anyway, we've got no time for your mysteries. We have work to do."

They went back to their lemonade stand. A police officer was waiting for them. Gwen poured him a big glass.

The officer took a huge gulp.

"AGGGHHHHH!" he cried, spitting it out. "Is this your idea of a joke?" He held his throat. "Give me something to drink! Quick!"

Hurriedly Jill poured another glass of lemonade.

"Not that poison," said the officer.

He ran down the street.

Gwen tasted the lemonade. "Yuck!" she cried. "It's full of pepper!"

Jill cautiously took a sip. "It is definitely pepper." She held the glass up to the sun and examined it. "But there are no black specks."

"Maybe you picked pepper leaves by mistake," suggested Gwen.

"We don't grow pepper leaves in our window box," said Jill. "But there's such a thing as white pepper. My mom and I use it for white sauces."

"Who cares about white sauces?" asked Gwen with a tap to her braces. "We have to find out who put pepper in our lemonade."

BLACK PEPPER BERRIES BEFORE THEY ARE GROUND

WHITE PEPPER IS BLACK PEPPER WITH THE BLACK HUSK REMOVED.

WHITE PEPPER IS USED IN WHITE SAUCES BECAUSE IT DOESN'T LEAVE BLACK SPECKS.

The Case of the White Pepper baffled Gwen all week, but she and Jill were so busy selling lemonade Gwen had little time to investigate.

MONDAY   TUESDAY AND WEDNESDAY   THURSDAY AND FRIDAY

One afternoon, during a lull when they finally had no customers, Jill noticed Fletcher was missing. "I haven't seen him since this morning," she said, sounding worried.

(FLETCHER'S ABSENCE)

Gwen and Jill searched for Fletcher. To their surprise they found him lying in Donald's empty wading pool, chewing on his favorite toy, a rubber salami that squeaked. Donald and his friends were nowhere to be seen.

"What are you doing in there?" exclaimed Jill.

Gwen picked up the rubber salami and gave it a squeak. "The last time Fletcher was missing . . ."

(FLETCHER'S RUBBER SALAMI)

Gwen didn't get to finish her sentence because a police car pulled up, full of thirsty officers, including Officer Malloy.

Each one bought a glass.

Suddenly one officer screamed, "THERE'S A GOLDFISH IN HERE!"

The officer dropped his glass, and a goldfish flopped onto Fletcher's back. Fletcher turned his head to see what it was.

"He's going to eat it!" warned Officer Malloy.

"I almost swallowed it!" said the officer whose cup it had been in.

Quickly Jill got some fresh water and put the goldfish into it.

"I think that was a very dumb joke," said the officer. He got back into the police car and the other officers followed.

Nobody paid.

Gwen tapped her braces. "Something *very, very queer* is going on."

"I won't argue with you," said Jill. She put her head halfway into the lemonade pitcher. "Hey, there's another one in here. These goldfish are the exact same color as our lemonade."

"First the pepper . . . and now the goldfish," mused Gwen. "Each time we left the pitcher alone for only a few minutes while we went to rescue Fletcher."

FRESH
WATER ---->

Gwen scratched Fletcher's belly. "Somebody is using Fletcher to get us out of the lemonade business. He or she lures Fletcher away, and while we look for Fletcher the dirty dope doctors our lemonade."

"We aren't going to sell much more lemonade if this keeps up," said Jill.

Gwen stared at the goldfish swimming happily in the fresh water. "Maybe we can trace the goldfish," she said. "Let's take them to the pet store."

ICE COL

They carried the glasses full of goldfish very carefully to the pet store around the corner. Ms. Hennessey, the owner, took one look at Fletcher and the goldfish and said, "No returns."

"I'd never return Fletcher," said Jill. "And we found the goldfish in our lemonade."

"Goldfish don't like lemonade," said Ms. Hennessey. "I'll sell you some goldfish food."

"You don't understand," said Gwen. She explained to Ms. Hennessey how the goldfish had mysteriously turned up in their lemonade.

DANA   GEORGE   DONALD

"Did you sell any goldfish like these in the last few days?" asked Gwen.

Ms. Hennessey thought for a moment. "I had three customers for goldfish yesterday: Dana Langer, George Ross, and Donald Payson."

"Donald and Dana!" cried Jill. "They were at the scene of the crime."

"And George Ross lives around the corner," said Gwen. "We'll ask each of them to show us the goldfish. If one of them doesn't have any goldfish and cooks with white pepper, we'll know who did it."

Ms. Hennessey looked confused.

George Ross lived the closest to the pet store. He was getting ready for a run. "I bought those silly goldfish for my sister for her birthday," he explained.

"Do you still have them?" asked Gwen.

"I told you," said George. "I gave them to her."

Gwen tapped her braces. But just then Carole, George's little sister, came home. When asked, she proudly showed Gwen and Jill her goldfish.

Gwen crossed George off her list.

The Langers lived on Follen Street. As Gwen and Jill turned the corner they saw a sign, DANA & ERICA LANGER'S FANTASTIC LEMONADE.

"They have a lemonade stand too!" cried Jill. "They stole our idea, and now they're trying to drive us out of business."

"You're right," said Gwen. "It had to be them. They were there right from the beginning!"

Gwen went straight up to Dana and said, "You . . . you put pepper and goldfish in our lemonade."

"What are you talking about?" asked Dana.

"Show us your goldfish if you're innocent," insisted Gwen.

"LOOK, BRACES-MOUTH," said Dana angrily, "I bought those goldfish with money I made from selling my excellent lemonade!"

Dana and Erica marched Gwen and Jill into the house and showed them Dana's goldfish swimming in their bowl.

"Uh, they're awfully nice goldfish," stammered Jill.

Gwen tapped her braces. "That leaves Donald with the only unaccounted-for goldfish," she said with a tap.

"What is TINSEL TEETH talking about?" asked Erica.

"Stop calling her names!" said Jill.

Gwen and Jill went back to see Donald. Dana and Erica insisted on following. "We want to get to the bottom of this too!" said Dana.

Gwen tapped her braces all the way. "Goldfish are not tropical fish," she whispered to Jill.

"Thank you," said Jill. "I'm glad you pointed that out."

"Don't be sarcastic," whispered Gwen. "Why would Donald buy goldfish if he collects rare tropical fish?"

Donald was in his backyard, standing on his platform with a hose in his hand. His tropical fish were all spread out in different small bowls on a picnic table. Donald seemed surprised to see Dana and Erica with Gwen and Jill. "I'm about to fill my aquarium," he said.

Just then they heard a car horn. A police car drove up.

"You have customers," said Donald.

Gwen looked closely at the fish on the picnic table. "Are these all your fish?" she asked.

"Yes," said Donald. "I'm putting my whole collection on display."

Gwen tapped her braces. "There are no gold-fish here. Yet, you bought goldfish yesterday."

She climbed the ladder to confront Donald. Fletcher and Jill followed her.

Gwen reached the top rung. "Have you been trying to put us out of business?" Gwen asked.

"Did you put pepper and goldfish in our lemonade?" demanded Jill.

Instead of answering, Donald aimed the hose right at Gwen. The water hit her in the face, and she and Fletcher tumbled into the pool.

"You . . . you . . ." sputtered Gwen. Donald jumped off his platform.

"AFTER HIM!" shouted Gwen, jumping out of the pool.

She, Jill, and Fletcher chased Donald all around his backyard, round and round the picnic table filled with Sailfin Mollies and Neon Tetras.

Dana and Erica stood to the side and watched.

Suddenly Donald slipped on the wet grass. He bumped into the picnic table and sent his tropical fish flying. Fletcher gawked, fascinated by the flip-flopping fish. He wagged his tail at them.

"OH NO!" yelled Donald. "My
fish! HELP! HELP! DON'T LET
THEM DIE!"

"You're a turkey," said Gwen, "but
your fish never hurt anyone." She
and Jill helped Donald rescue all his fish.

Dana and Erica still did nothing.

One Sailfin Molly fell right next to the platform. Gwen knelt to pick it up. She saw "Police Dept. Property" stamped on one of the boards.

"You got these boards from the old police station, didn't you?" asked Gwen. Then she looked puzzled.

"But I still don't understand why you tried to drive us out of business. You'd better tell me, or I won't give you back your Sailfin Molly."

"Blackmail," said Donald.

"It's not blackmail!" said Gwen.
"You're the one who put pepper and
goldfish in our lemonade."

"I didn't mean you," said Donald.
"Dana and Erica blackmailed me."

Dana and Erica tried to slink away,
but Fletcher was in their way.

Donald blushed brighter than a Neon Tetra. "Dana and Erica blackmailed me. They threatened to tell the police I had taken the old boards and bricks without asking. They were going to go to the cops unless I let them sell lemonade at my aquarium."

"But why did you have to put *us* out of business?" Gwen wanted to know.

"We get hardly any customers on our street," whined Dana. "We wanted to be the *only* lemonade stand near the aquarium. We made Donald try to put you out of business."

"When all the police started to buy your lemonade, I was sure they'd spot their lumber and bricks," said Donald. "I had to act."

"I should have thought of you," said Jill. "Your dad loves to cook. I bet he has white pepper."

"But the pepper didn't stop you, so I used goldfish," admitted Donald. "I was worried though. Lemonade isn't really good for goldfish."

"We never meant for you to put pepper and goldfish in their lemonade," said Erica. "We thought you could just tell them they'd have to close shop."

"Well, how was I going to do that?" shouted Donald. "It's a free country!"

"And we're not afraid of competition," said Jill.

Dana and Erica looked even more embarrassed. "We were," said Erica.

Donald went to the police station and admitted taking the old bricks and wood. Officer Malloy told him that he should have asked permission.

In exchange for the wood and bricks Donald offered to let all the kids from the Police Athletic League into his aquarium for free, and he offered to teach them about tropical fish.

Once DONALD'S ASTOUNDING AQUARIUM opened, Gwen and Jill were busier than ever.

Although they let Dana and Erica *try* to sell lemonade, most people wanted FLETCHER'S FABULOUS LEMONADE because it was made with fresh lemons. Dana and Erica used a mix.

Fletcher discovered a new hobby. He loved to lie down in the shade and watch the fish swim round and round in circles.

FLETCHER'S FABULOUS LEMONADE

TO MAKE 4½ QUARTS

SQUEEZE 12 LEMONS. SAVE 2 OF THE
SQUEEZED-OUT LEMONS.
ADD 1 POUND OF SUGAR TO THE
LEMON JUICE.

Note: The secret of great lemonade is to add
the sugar to the lemon juice *before*
you add the water.

OPTIONAL: Grate the rind (the yellow part
of the peel) of the 2 lemons
you have saved.

Note: This is hard, but it adds zest to the
lemonade. In fact, the lemon peel is
sometimes called zest.

Put everything into a quart jar and seal.

WHEN READY TO SERVE AND MAKE
MONEY ADD 4 QUARTS OF ICE WATER
AND 12 MINT LEAVES. IF YOU DON'T
HAVE MINT LEAVES, THIS LEMONADE
WILL BE PRETTY FABULOUS ANYWAY.

CELEBRATING

YEARLING
25 YEARS

Yearling Books
celebrates its
25 years—
and salutes
Reading Is
Fundamental®
on its 25th
anniversary.